F
Hat
Hatcher, Robin Lee
Sweet Dreams Drive

## DATE DUE

| MAY 1 5 2007 | | |
|---|---|---|
| MAY 2 3 2007 | | |
| JUN 0 8 2007 | | |
| JUN 2 5 2007 | | |
| JUL 2 1 2007 | | |
| JUL 2 6 2007 | | |
| AUG 1 4 2007 | | |
| SEP 0 5 2007 | | |
| SEP 2 1 2007 | | |
| NOV 1 7 2007 | | |
| JUL 3 1 2008 | | |
| OCT 2 7 2010 | | |

## Praise for Other Books in the Hart's Crossing Series

"Robin Lee Hatcher has a way of telling a story that makes you feel the characters are your own family. *Legacy Lane* is a wonderful story full of the warmth and charm of a Sunday afternoon in the country. Don't miss this one—you'll want to linger over each page."

—Colleen Coble, author of *Without a Trace*

"Once readers step into the engaging town of Hart's Crossing, they're hooked. The scenes come to life, leading readers on a tender journey of God's amazing forgiveness and grace. You'll want to return for another delightful visit."

—Gail Gaymer Martin, author of *The Christmas Kite*

"With *Legacy Lane*, Robin Lee Hatcher again proves why her books are so anticipated and appreciated. Robin brings us a tender story about real flesh and blood people, small-town neighbors with big hearts, and a mother's love."

—Lorena McCourtney, author of the Julesburg Mysteries series and *Invisible*

"Robin Lee Hatcher's *Legacy Lane*, a gentle story of an awakening soul, will touch hearts. It touched mine."

—Lyn Cote, author of *Winter's Secret*

"Robin Lee Hatcher has written a delightful, grace-filled story of a young woman's search for meaning in life and a place to belong. The citizens of Hart's Crossing gently show the way to both. *Legacy Lane* is a wonderful beginning to a promising new series."

—Deborah Raney, author of *A Nest of Sparrows* and *Playing by Heart*

"Robin Lee Hatcher's visit to *Legacy Lane* is like going home for the holidays! It's warm, cozy, and filled with charm. Curl up and enjoy!"

—Kristin Billerbeck, author of *What a Girl Wants*

Sweet
Dreams
Drive

# Sweet Dreams Drive

HART'S CROSSING SERIES #4

ROBIN LEE HATCHER

Revell
Grand Rapids, Michigan

Published by Fleming H. Revell
a division of Baker Publishing Group
P.O. Box 6287, Grand Rapids, MI 49516-6287
www.revellbooks.com

Printed in the United States of America

Library of Congress Cataloging-in-Publication Data
Hatcher, Robin Lee.
    Sweet Dreams Drive / Robin Lee Hatcher.
        p.    cm. — (Hart's Crossing series; #4)
    ISBN 10: 0-8007-1857-7 (cloth)
    ISBN 978-0-8007-1857-2 (cloth)
    1. Married people—Fiction. 2. Parenthood—Fiction. 3. Infants—
Fiction. 4. Twins—Fiction. I. Title.
PS3558.A73574S94  2007
813'.54—dc22                                              2007000874

Scripture is taken from the *Holy Bible*, New Living Translation, copyright © 1996. Used by permission of Tyndale House Publishers, Inc., Wheaton, Illinois 60189. All rights reserved.

To my wonderful Revell editors,
Jennifer and Kristin.
Thanks for going the extra mile.

# PROLOGUE

The sanctuary of the Hart's Crossing Community Church was draped with blue satin and white netting. Candles flickered in candelabras. Soft music from the organ drifted to the rafters as guests were ushered down the aisle.

As a friend of the bride, Patti Sinclair sat on the left side of the church, although in a town this size, it didn't matter. Everybody pretty much knew everybody. Patti hadn't lived in Hart's Crossing in seven years, but she had no trouble picking out familiar faces among the guests.

Close to the front sat Till Hart, the unofficial grandmother of the town. Hart's Crossing was named for one of her ancestors. Miss Hart had the sweetest smile and kindest eyes of anyone Patti knew.

Next to Till sat Francine Hunter, Chuck and Steph Watson, and Ethel Jacobsen. The four women were all part of a group of quilters. What did they call themselves? The Huckleberries? No, that wasn't it. She smiled as the name came to her. The Thimbleberries. The Thimbleberry Quilting Club.

Amazing that she could remember it all these years later.

One row behind the quilters were Nancy and Harry Raney. Who could forget the owners of the Over the Rainbow Diner? That was *the* place to hang out when she was a teenager. The only place.

She saw Police Chief Coble a couple rows further back. Who was that blonde beside him? Could that be his daughter? The last time Patti saw her, Cassandra had been a gawky kid in middle school. No more.

The music changed. Patti looked over her shoulder to see the mother of the bride being escorted down the aisle. Patti's gaze shifted to the usher. The church went silent, and the world shifted on its axis.

10

The ceremony was half over before Patti fully recovered.

The wedding reception was held outdoors at Hart's Crossing's golf course. Patti congratulated the bride—Olivia, her best friend in elementary school—and the groom before moving to the refreshment table, where she was handed a cup of punch.

"Patti Sinclair. Is that you?"

She turned to see another familiar face.

"I'm Eric Bedford. Remember me?"

"Of course. You played the drums in the middle school band one year. That was the year Toby Kasner broke your nose with a drumstick."

"Ouch." He touched the bridge of his nose. "I'd almost forgotten."

"I'll never forget. Blood gushed everywhere. It was like a war zone."

He laughed, then asked, "So where are you living now?"

"Nampa. How about you?"

11

"Right here. The old Bedford roots go pretty deep. Dad's still farming. My brother got his degree and is teaching school here." His eyebrows raised. "Speak of the devil. Hey, Al. Come over here."

Patti turned her head, ready to greet Eric's brother, and the earth tilted for the second time that day. That golden hair. Those green eyes. That crooked smile. Those broad shoulders.

"Al, this is Patti Sinclair. She used to live in Hart's Crossing. Did you two ever meet?"

"Not sure. Maybe." Al held out his hand. "Nice to see you again, Patti."

If they'd met before, Patti would remember. Either that or Al Bedford had changed a lot in the past seven years.

Eric said, "She's living in Nampa."

"Do you like it there?"

She nodded, tongue-tied and breathless.

"Care to sit down?" Al asked.

"That would be nice." Hopefully, she could walk on her rubbery legs.

She didn't know what happened to Eric. By the time she and Al reached one of the white plastic tables placed under a large canopy, Al's younger brother was no longer around. Just as well, since the table Al chose had only two chairs. He held one for her.

So he was a gentleman as well as handsome. When was the last time she'd stumbled upon that combination?

"What do you do in Nampa?" Al sat in the other chair.

"I'm an editor at a small publishing house. I was hired part time while in college, and they offered me a full-time position after I graduated."

"Do you like it?"

"Yes." The way he watched her made her insides go all aflutter. She lowered her gaze to her hands. "Eric says you're a teacher. What subject?"

"Everything. I teach sixth graders at the elementary school."

His answer surprised her. For some reason, she'd expected him to say history or algebra or some other class taught at the high school level.

She asked another question. He answered and asked his own.

Patti shared about her mom's divorce when she was

in middle school. Al shared about the recent death of his grandfather, a farmer like his dad. She shared about her move to Boise at the age of sixteen and how difficult it had been to feel comfortable with city life, though she loved it now. He shared how eager he'd been to finish college and get his teaching certificate so he could return to Hart's Crossing. She shared her love of books and the theater. He shared his passion for golf and basketball. She mentioned her cat. He told funny stories about his dog.

And in the midst of it all, there came a moment when Patti knew that Al Bedford was destined to be part of her future. At least, she hoped so with all her heart.

# CHAPTER ONE

**Four Years Later**

Soft mewling sounds awakened Patti at 3:00 a.m. She lay still, hoping Al would get up and be able to walk the baby back to sleep. Trouble was, if she waited too long, the cries of one twin would wake the other.

She heard Al's breathing, a sound not quite a snore but close enough. As she slipped from beneath the sheet and lightweight blanket, she felt a spark of irritation. Not at their precious twins, but at her husband. Why did he get to sleep when she didn't?

The two bassinets—one pink, one blue—were set

in the far corner of the master bedroom. Moonlight, falling through the window, illuminated her way across the room. Placing one hand on each bassinet, she leaned over to see which baby was fussing. Like his father, Weston didn't budge. Sunni, however, punched the air with tiny fists, warming up for a good cry.

"Shh," Patti whispered as she lifted her infant daughter. "Mommy's here. Shh."

A short while later, as the baby nursed at her breast, Patti set the rocking chair in motion and stared out the window of the family room. The silvery-white moonlight bathed the rooftop of the house across the back fence. Somewhere in the neighborhood, a dog barked. Soon another dog replied. It was a strangely comforting sound.

She and Al had purchased this home in a new subdivision on the east side of Hart's Crossing last spring. She'd fallen in love with it upon entering through the front door. If they were going to stay in this small town, then this was the home she wanted to live in. Yes, the mortgage was higher than what they wanted, but whose wasn't? At least they were investing their money instead of throwing it away on rent. She just wished there was a little more of Al's paycheck left over each month after they paid their bills.

She leaned her head against the back of the rocker and closed her eyes as the memory of their latest argument played through her head.

*"We could move to Boise. You'd make more money in a larger school district, and you'd have more opportunities for advancement."*

*"There's more to life than money, Patti. I want our kids to grow up in Hart's Crossing. We've talked about that. I like my job. I like the people I work with. I know and love the kids I teach. There's no reason to leave."*

*"Raising children is expensive. Have you seen the doctor and hospital bills?"*

*"We'll manage."*

Tears spilled from beneath her eyelids, trailing down her cheeks. She and Al never used to fight. Now they seemed to disagree about everything. Her mother said it was whacked-out hormones and too little sleep. Maybe that was true. Maybe not.

Her gaze lowered to the infant in her arms. Sunni slept again, her mouth gone slack.

*Why can't I be content with things as they are?*

Guilt surged. She had much to be thankful for. And she *was* thankful. Truly, she was. The babies were healthy and strong despite their early arrival. Al loved teaching at Hart's Crossing Elementary. Her wonderful mother-in-law dropped by as often as she could to help with the twins. The ladies of the Thimbleberry Quilting Club and her friends from church had showered the Bedford family with gifts.

And yet . . .

*I'm sorry, God. I don't mean to complain.*

There was something else to feel guilty over. Her spiritual walk was almost nonexistent, except for church on Sundays. For several years it had been her habit to rise early to read her Bible and pray before she got ready for work. She'd loved those quiet times, sitting in the Lord's presence, waiting for him to speak to her heart. When was the last time she'd read her Bible? When was the last time she'd heard God's voice? Weeks? No. More like months.

With a sigh, she rose from the rocker and carried the baby to the pink bassinet in the bedroom.

*If I just weren't so tired all the time, maybe—*

As if on cue, Weston whimpered.

Patti cast an envious glance toward her sleeping husband before stepping toward the blue bassinet.

The *beep-beep* of the alarm clock awakened Al at 6:30. With a flailing arm, he managed to hit the snooze button without opening his eyes. He wanted five more minutes of sleep, and he didn't need the alarm waking the twins.

This first week of the new school year had been rough. In the past, he'd looked forward to meeting his students and discovering more about each one of them, but he hadn't had much rest since the babies were born. A sleep-deprived teacher had few defenses against the wiles of a bunch of sixth graders still getting into the groove after summer vacation.

"Al?"

So much for those last five minutes. "Hmm."

"I didn't make your sandwich last night. I forgot."

He opened his eyes. Morning light filtered through the bedroom curtains. "That's okay. I'll get hot lunch with the kids. I think it's burger day." He turned his head on the pillow to look at his wife. Her eyes were closed.

"I was up and down with the babies three times in the night." Patti pulled the sheet over her head as she rolled onto her side. "Try not to wake them."

"I'll do my best."

He slid out of bed and made his way to the master bathroom, closing the door without a sound. He didn't bother to flip the light switch. Enough daylight came through the block-glass window over the jetted tub.

Minutes later, freshly shaved, he stood beneath the shower spray, suds from the shampoo sliding in globs down his cheeks and neck as he used the bar of soap to lather the rest of his body. He wasn't normally a guy who took long showers, but this morning he had to resist the desire to stand there, eyes closed, and catch those five extra minutes of sleep.

But he didn't. Duty called—and so did eighteen eleven-year-olds.

After dressing in clothes he'd laid out the night before, he left the bathroom and walked to the edge of the bed, where he leaned down and kissed his wife on the forehead. Next he moved to the bassinets, where he smiled at his son and daughter, so sweet in slumber.

*See you tonight*, he mouthed before leaving the bedroom.

Al was thankful the twins had arrived during the summer months. It had given him time to bond with them in a way many dads couldn't because of their work schedules. He didn't mind changing diapers or burping or bathing them. The only thing he couldn't do was feed them. And even though there were times he might prefer his children had arrived one at a time, with a couple years in between, he wouldn't trade Sunni and Weston for a million bucks.

He yawned as he grabbed his briefcase and car keys from the table near the back door, already planning to get a few minutes of shut-eye during the lunch break.

# CHAPTER TWO

Honey," her mother said, "it's time you found someone to watch the babies and give yourself a few hours out of the house."

"How can I do that?" Patti shifted the cordless handset to her left ear and pressed it close with her shoulder, then continued folding towels. "Do you know how much sitters want per hour these days? Even in a small town like this one."

"Are you telling me you have no friends who would watch those adorable babies for a couple of hours?"

"Of course I have friends who would do it if I asked. But I think they're intimidated by two babies." *I know I am sometimes.* "I'd hate to impose on them." She released a sigh. "I wish you could have stayed in Hart's Crossing longer."

"Me too. But I've used the last of my vacation time for this year."

"I know." She swallowed another sigh.

"You heed my words. Get out of the house for a while. Even if it's just long enough to get yourself a cup of coffee at the diner. You'll have a better perspective on things if you do."

Her mother made it sound so easy. If only . . .

"I've got to run, dear. I'm about to burn your stepfather's dinner."

"Bye, Mom. Give Doug my love."

"I will. You do the same with Al."

After setting aside the phone, Patti sank onto a chair at the kitchen table. Wouldn't she love to take her mom's advice? How much fun it would be to go down to Twin Falls to spend a few hours at the mall. Or maybe drive up to the resort for a nice dinner with her husband. It felt as if she and Al hadn't talked to each other in ages, other than to say, "Would you change her diaper?" or "Can you fold the laundry?" or "Where's dinner?"

Or to argue. Again.

And though she was loathe to admit it, she started too many of those arguments. What was wrong with her? Why did she pick fights with him? It wasn't for sport. She preferred peace. She preferred laughter.

Patti swept loose strands of hair back from her face as her gaze moved around the kitchen. Breakfast dishes were in the sink, and the dishwasher needed to be emptied. Clean baby clothes, sheets, and towels—about four loads' worth of laundry—had yet to be folded. Al would be home in less than an hour, and she hadn't given a thought to dinner. Was anything defrosted?

After she and Al moved into their new home last March, Patti had kept everything in perfect order. Little Miss Susie Homemaker. That was Patti. She loved cleaning and shining and decorating, and her pregnancy hadn't slowed her down one bit. She couldn't have imagined the day would come when her home looked like a cyclone hit it.

She heard a knock on the back door and turned to see who it was. Amy Livingston, the thirteen-year-old girl from next door, grinned and waved at her through the glass.

25

"Come in, Amy. It's unlocked."

The girl opened the door. "Hey, Mrs. Bedford. How're the twins today?"

"They're sleeping." She glanced at the baby monitor on the counter. Not a sound came through the speaker, to her great relief.

"Mom said it was okay if I came over as long as I'm not in the way. Will I be in the way? Can I help with something?"

"Amy, you're a lifesaver. I could definitely use some help. Would you mind folding the laundry while I clean the kitchen and see what I can fix Al for dinner?"

"No, I don't mind. Is there any special way you fold things?"

Patti laughed. "Any way that gets it done is okay with me."

She rose from the chair and moved toward the dishwasher. In short order, she had the clean dishes in the cupboards and the dirty ones closed inside the machine. Then, with a bottle of spray cleaner in one hand and a damp cloth in the other, she wiped the countertops, the front of the microwave, and the handles on the refrigerator.

She was staring into the pantry, contemplating dinner, when she heard the first whimper through the monitor. The fullness in her breasts told her it was feeding time. It looked like Al would have to wait for his supper again.

"Hey, Bedford!"

Standing beside his 1991 Alfa Romeo Spider convertible—a college graduation gift from his parents—Al looked over his shoulder and watched as Jeff Cavanaugh, the town doctor, strode toward him.

"What's up, Doc?"

Jeff rolled his eyes at Al's Bugs Bunny impersonation—an old and overused joke—and ignored the question. "You look tired, buddy."

"Yeah, it's hard to remember what a good night's sleep feels like."

"But your babies are thriving. I was pleased when they were in for their six-week checkup."

"That's what Patti said."

27

Jeff jerked his head toward the building. "I'd better get inside. I promised Penny I'd help her with a school project her first graders are doing." He flexed his right arm. "I'm the muscle."

"Things getting serious between you two?"

"Could be." Jeff shrugged.

Love was definitely in the air in Hart's Crossing. Al and Patti had been to two weddings in the past nine months. First there was James Scott and Steph Watson, childhood sweethearts who'd fallen in love again after fifty years apart. They'd wed in late autumn, before the first snows flew. In May, Angie Hunter and Bill Palmer, owner of the local weekly newspaper, tied the knot in a ceremony with the whole town turned out to witness the union. Now word was Mel Jenkins had proposed to Terri Sampson, the mother of one of Al's current students, and the wedding was set to take place in December.

Yes, love was in the air. Why not for Jeff and Penny?

Al opened the car door and tossed his briefcase onto the passenger seat. "Cavanaugh, you're the most eligible bachelor this town's got left. Good looking and a doctor to boot. What mother wouldn't want you for her daughter? I'd say your days are numbered."

Jeff gave him a good-natured punch in the shoulder, then walked toward the main entrance to the school.

On the drive home, Al's thoughts drifted to the day he and Patti first met. He'd been taken with her from the start. Lucky he hadn't tripped as he walked Olivia's mother to her seat at the front of the church. In the months that followed, he made countless trips to Nampa, about a three-and-a-half hour drive from Hart's Crossing. The more he saw her, the more he knew he wanted to spend his life with her. One of the best days of his life was when he proposed and she said yes.

Maybe Patti was right. Maybe he should look for work outside of Hart's Crossing. His teaching salary was stretched to the limit with a wife, two babies, payments on a used Honda Odyssey, and a hefty mortgage. Only he didn't want to leave his hometown. Patti knew that was how he felt before they got married. She'd been in agreement with him. At least, that's what she'd told him in the beginning.

Approaching their house on White Cloud Drive, Al pushed the button on the remote clipped to the visor, slowed as the garage door opened, then drove in beside the Odyssey. He glanced at the front yard as he exited the car. The lawn needed to be mowed, but he wasn't keen on doing it with the temperature still hovering around the ninety-degree mark. Cooler weather couldn't get here fast enough to suit him.

As he opened the door into the house, he called, "I'm home."

A moment later, Amy Livingston poked her head into the kitchen. "Hi, Mr. Bedford. Mrs. Bedford's upstairs feeding the twins. I was on my way home." She waved before making a beeline for the back patio door. "Bye!"

"See ya."

Two years ago, Amy had been one of his students. She was bright, friendly, and as kids her age go, dependable. From the moment the Bedfords moved to this house, she'd been a presence in their lives. Maybe because she was an only child with a working mom and a father who traveled a lot for his business. Plus she was crazy about the twins.

She wasn't the only one who could say that.

Al dropped his briefcase near the entrance of the den before taking the stairs two at a time. He paused in the doorway of the master bedroom.

Patti sat in an overstuffed chair, her legs tucked to one side, one of the babies nursing at her breast. Her long, black, wavy hair was pulled into a ponytail, keeping it out of her face and out of reach of an infant's grasping fingers.

"Hey, beautiful."

She looked up with a smile. "I didn't hear you come in."

"I came in as Amy was leaving." He strode across the room to look at the baby in her arms. "Wes's turn?"

"Mmm. Sunni ate first."

He stepped to the side of the pink bassinet. His daughter stared up at him with wide, dark eyes. "Aren't you supposed to be sleepy after you eat?" He lifted her into his arms and kissed the top of her downy-haired head.

Did every dad feel like his heart might explode with joy when he held his child? There wasn't anything like this. Nothing to compare.

"Al, I've been thinking I might want to start supplementing with formula."

"Really?" He turned to look at Patti.

"I'm not sure I'm making enough milk."

"Jeff said their weight's good."

Tears flooded her eyes and slipped down her cheeks. She lowered her gaze to Weston, but not before Al felt like a complete heel for making her cry—even though he didn't know what he'd said wrong.

"Patti, I thought breast-feeding was the better way to go. That's all."

"Better for you, maybe," she said softly.

"What?"

"Nothing." She shook her head. "I'm sorry. I'm just tired."

Al sank onto the ottoman near the chair. "Hey, if you think that's what you should do—"

"I don't know what I think I should do." She met his gaze again, giving him a tremulous smile. "I love the ease of nursing, and I know it's better for them.

I've tried using that pump I got at my baby shower, but . . . Oh, I don't know. I just feel like if the twins were on bottles, things would be easier. We could even ask someone to watch them for a little while. Maybe you and I could go to dinner or to a movie instead of staying home all the time." Patti moved Weston to her shoulder and started patting his back. "Would you order a pizza to be delivered?"

Pizza? That was the fourth time in two weeks.

Al swallowed his objection. His wife was in one of those moods, and he didn't want to make her cry again.

"Sure. I'll call it in now." He glanced at the baby in the crook of his arm. "Come on, Sunni. You can help me decide what to get."

# CHAPTER THREE

Patti paused a moment in her housecleaning to watch Al as he mowed the back lawn. A blue baseball cap covered his blond hair and shaded his eyes from the sun as he strode toward the east. Clad in a loose tank top and khaki shorts, he walked with a long, easy gait, his bare legs and arms tanned to a dark bronze after a summer of yard work.

Most Saturdays the hum of his mower was one of several. But on this first weekend in September, many of their neighbors were gone for the final three-day holiday of summer, leaving the neighborhood oddly silent.

Last Labor Day weekend, she and Al had borrowed

a tent trailer from a friend and gone camping in Grand Teton National Park. During the days, they hiked trails, rode horses, and ate copious amounts of food. At night, they huddled together near the campfire and talked about their future and what God might have in store for them.

That was the same weekend Patti first suggested they should start a family. Her job with the publishing company, which she'd been able to continue after their wedding via telecommuting, had ended due to in-house changes. Maybe now, she'd said, was the time to think about having children of their own. She hadn't shared with Al that her heart longed to be part of a family, a family that was whole, where the husband loved his wife, the dad loved his kids. She hadn't told him because it was a truth she barely acknowledged to herself.

The doorbell rang, drawing her thoughts to the present. She hurried to answer it.

Sven Johnson, the mailman, stood on the front porch. Grizzled, gray-haired, and bent at the shoulders, he smiled at her through thick spectacles. "Morning, Patricia."

"Good morning, Mr. Johnson."

"Have a package for you." He held a box toward her, the rest of the mail stacked on top of it.

"Thanks." She took hold of the items with both hands.

"Give my best to Alfred."

She swallowed a chuckle. No one but Sven called Al by his given name. "I'll do it."

As soon as the door closed, she carried the mail into the kitchen and set it on the table. The return label on the box told her these must be the books she had ordered a week ago. She grabbed a knife from the drawer and sliced open the packing tape.

"Wow," she whispered as she pulled the first of two coffee-table books free of its wrapping. "It's even more beautiful than I expected." She flipped through the pages, admiring the nature photos, reading the captions.

"What's that?" Al asked from the back doorway.

She set the book on the table and closed its cover before looking in his direction. "The mail. Mr. Johnson brought it to the door."

Al removed his grass-stained athletic shoes before entering the house. "I meant the book."

"Oh, it's the most beautiful collection of photographs from around the world. The captions are all Bible verses. I bought the pair for the coffee table in the living room."

He looked at her for a few moments before picking up the receipt. "Forty dollars?"

"That includes the shipping. They were marked way down. I saved 50 percent."

"We didn't *need* them, Patti."

She sent him a glare that told him what she thought of his tone.

Al let the receipt float to the table before stepping toward the sink to wash his hands. Patti stared at his back, all the while hoping one of the twins would cry so she would have an excuse to leave. She didn't want to continue this conversation. It would lead to another argument, the same old argument they'd had for months.

But no sounds came through the baby monitor. She was stuck where she was.

Drying his hands on a dishtowel, Al turned to face

her. "Honey, I know you want our home to look nice. So do I. But we've got to stick to our budget." He spoke slowly, as if afraid she wouldn't understand. "We're already carrying too high of a balance on our credit cards. The interest is killing us. We're barely touching the principal each month."

She wasn't a complete fool. She knew their finances were stretched to the limit. But sometimes she wanted to buy things because she *liked* them, not because they were a necessity. Was that so terrible? Did her whole world have to consist of diapers and laundry soap? Couldn't he cut her some slack? Didn't he know she did it for him?

There was a time when Al thought that stubborn tilt of Patti's chin was adorable. Not so much lately.

"You know what?" He tossed the towel onto the counter. "Maybe *you* ought to pay the bills for the next month and see what it's like. Maybe then you wouldn't be so quick to order things we don't need or to order pizza delivered two nights a week."

"I could do as good a job as you're doing, *Alfred* Bedford. And without so much bellyaching."

Al clenched his jaw. He didn't want to say something he would have to apologize for later.

"But if I'm paying the bills, buster, you can take care of the babies while I do it."

"You mean, take care of them without so much bellyaching?"

Her eyes went wide, and her mouth formed an *O* as she sucked in air.

Well, now he'd gone and done it. Said something he'd have to apologize for. But he wasn't apologizing right now. "I need gas for the mower. Be back in a while."

He was still mad when he pulled up to the pump at the Main Street Service Station ten minutes later.

"Women," he muttered as he opened the driver's side door.

He retrieved the gas can from the back of the minivan—no way did he haul gas in his sports car—and set it next to the pump. Straightening, he pulled his wallet from his back pocket and checked to see how much cash he had. After the words he'd exchanged with his wife, he preferred not to use the credit card.

Three bucks. That should get him through the last mowing of the year. He lifted the nozzle for regular gasoline and stuck it into the can.

He shouldn't have said what he had to Patti. He should have kept his temper in check. He knew she was tired. She didn't get enough sleep. But neither did he, and he had to face a classroom of eleven- and twelve-year-olds five days a week. She didn't have to go to an office every day where someone judged her performance.

Besides, Patti was the one who'd wanted to buy the new house. He would have been just as happy with something smaller and less expensive in an older part of town. He'd told her they would have to cut corners if they bought the new house, and she'd agreed to it.

Lost in thought, he was past the three-dollar mark before he realized it. "Idiot." Now he would have to use his credit card.

He saw himself in his mind, scowling at the gas can while talking under his breath. He acted like charging three dollars and twenty-seven cents was the end of the world.

Recalling what he'd said to Patti before storming out of the house, his amusement faded. He'd hurt her, and that wasn't funny. It didn't matter if he had cause to be angry. He shouldn't have said what he did.

He needed to get home and apologize. Fast.

Patti hid her face in her folded arms on top of the kitchen table, the sound of the slamming door echoing in her mind. Her chest ached.

*Oh, God. What's wrong with me?*

She recalled another slamming door, the one that closed behind her father the day he walked out for good. Her parents had fought a lot too. Her childhood home had been filled with tension whenever her parents were together. Even at thirteen, Patti had promised herself that when she got married her home would be different. She would make it a haven for her family.

What if she drove Al away, spending money she shouldn't, getting angry at the drop of a hat? What if he walked out that door and never came back?

She heard the garage door open. Seconds passed, counted by the ticking of the mantel clock.

"Patti?" Al stepped into the kitchen, stopping when he saw her at the table. "Patti, I'm sorry."

She rose from the chair. "Me too."

"I lost my temper and said things I shouldn't."

"I shouldn't have bought those books."

He moved toward her. She stepped into his arms, pressing her cheek against his chest.

"I'll curb my spending, Al. I promise."

"I love you. We'll be okay."

*Please, God. Let it be true.*

# CHAPTER FOUR

R emember to bring your permission slips to school tomorrow," Al called to his departing students the following Thursday.

Not that any of them listened. Once that dismissal bell sounded, they tuned him out. He'd been the same at their age.

After everyone was gone and he'd performed a quick sweep of the room to see if anything important was left behind, Al sank onto his desk chair and reached for the top paper in the stack of essays that awaited him. He liked to begin the year by asking his students to write about the favorite thing they did during the summer and three reasons why they liked it so much. Sure, it was a knock-off on "How I spent my summer vacation," but it worked. It helped him get to know the kids.

The first essay was by Lyssa Sampson. If he was a betting man, he'd wager hers was about Little League baseball. He would have lost that bet. She'd written about a camping trip with Mel Jenkins, her soon-to-be stepdad.

He smiled as he read the essay. Lyssa had a way with words that brought the vacation experience to life on the page. Her writing also made him see Mel, manager of the Farmers Independent Bank, in a whole new light. He hoped his own kids would write as affectionately about him when they were Lyssa's age.

His gaze drifted to the framed photo on his desk. In it, Patti sat on the living room sofa, holding a baby in each arm. The twins were about two weeks old at the time, their eyes closed and frowns creasing their brows, as if to say, "We don't want our picture taken." Hard to believe those two small bundles would be writing essays for their sixth-grade teacher eleven years from now.

He shook his head. Eleven years ago, he'd been a cocky college student, staying up too late, living on pizza and breakfast cereal. Despite his youthful antics, he'd managed to graduate with honors, but in the meantime, he was responsible for more than a few of his parents' gray hairs.

"Knock, knock."

He looked toward the classroom doorway. "Hey, Cassandra."

"Am I disturbing you?"

"Not really. What's up?"

Cassandra Coble—a tall, model-thin blonde—leaned her shoulder against the doorjamb and crossed one ankle over the other. "Nothing, really. I just needed to hear an adult's voice for a few minutes before I tackle my lesson plan."

"The natives restless today?"

"You said it. None of them seem able to concentrate. Their bodies are here, but their minds are elsewhere." She twirled a strand of pale gold hair with an index finger as she spoke.

Like Al, Cassandra grew up in Hart's Crossing, but she was seven years younger, so he hadn't come to know her until she returned to town last year with her degree and was hired to teach fifth graders in the room next to his.

"Another week, and they'll settle into the routine," he said, leaning back in his chair.

"I hope you're right." She laughed softly. "Were they like this last year?"

"They're like this at the start of every school year."

"I guess I was too excited about my new job to notice."

"Probably."

She pointed toward his desk. "Is that a new photo of the twins?"

"No. Same one."

"You ought to have Walt Foster come over to take some family photos. He's a great photographer."

The cell phone on Al's desk vibrated, drawing his gaze. Seeing his home number in the ID, he picked up the phone and flipped it open. "Hey, hon."

"Did I call too soon?"

"No. The kids are long gone. I was just talking with one of the other teachers."

Cassandra straightened away from the doorjamb, gave him a smile and a little wave, then disappeared from view.

"We're invited to a party at Jeff's house on Saturday. He and Penny are having a group of friends over for a game night. I hope it's all right that I said we could go."

"What about the babies?"

"Jeff said to bring them along. If they're fussy, we'll have plenty of people there to help."

"You sure you want to go?" He thought of how much stuff they would have to take with them. Was it worth it for a few hours playing Scene It or Cranium?

She laughed. "I'm sure. I'm ready for some fun. Getting more rest has made a world of difference."

Over the past week, the twins had slept for longer stretches at night, a change that had improved the moods of both parents.

"So what do you say, Al?"

"Sure. Why not?"

After hanging up the phone, Patti hurried into the walk-in closet to look for something to wear on Saturday. She'd lost a good portion of her baby weight but not enough to squeeze into her favorite jeans.

"I need to diet," she whispered as she slid hanger after hanger along the rod. Things either didn't fit or were out of season or out of style.

Maybe she could run down to Yvonne's Boutique on Saturday morning and find a nice pair of jeans that wouldn't make her look too fat. As quickly as the thought came, she discarded it. The boutique didn't have much in the way of fashionable jeans, and even if they did, Al would have a fit about the cost.

She sighed. She would have to make do with what she had.

If only Al wasn't such a penny-pincher. She hadn't expected that of him when they were courting. Why would she when he drove to Nampa often, taking her to movies and to dinner, buying her gifts? Of course, back then he lived in a basement apartment, drove a car that was over two decades old, and carried a zero balance on his one and only credit card. Now he had a family of four to support.

*He does the best he can.*

She shook her head. Al wasn't a penny-pincher. It was unfair to think such things about him. He was a good provider, a good husband, a good father.

Patti left the walk-in and headed out of the bedroom, hoping the twins would sleep another thirty minutes. That would give her time to start dinner. She'd almost reached the kitchen when the doorbell rang.

*Please don't wake the babies.*

She opened the front door as the UPS truck pulled away from the curb. On the stoop was a box. She leaned forward to see who it was from: Sweet Baby Things.

"Oh no."

She'd forgotten. Completely and totally forgotten. Last weekend, around four o'clock on Saturday morning, upset with Al, unable to sleep, continuing to debate adding formula to the twins' diet, she'd found this breast-pump system while browsing online. "Amazing!" the consumer reviews said. "The most advanced system available to mothers," the manufacturer promised.

*"Patti, I thought breast-feeding was the better way to go."* That's what Al had said the day before she ordered the pump. He hadn't wanted her to stop nursing the babies.

And so she ordered the fancy pump.

For $320, plus tax and shipping.

Her stomach churned as she lifted the box and carried it inside.

She'd meant to tell him about it the day she ordered it. Really, she had. But how could she, after he made such a big deal over the forty dollars she spent for those books? And when they made up after the fight, she didn't want to spoil things again. So she'd waited.

Now they had plans for an evening of fun. She didn't want to spoil that either. No, she would have to wait a little longer. Another couple of days wouldn't matter that much. Monday. She could tell him on Monday.

She carried the box upstairs and stuck it in the corner of the closet.

# CHAPTER FIVE

Patti chose a frilly pink dress with matching tights and a bonnet with white lace trim for her daughter to wear on Saturday evening. For her son, she chose a tiny pair of jeans with a blue shirt and suspenders.

"Look at you, little cowboy." She held Weston up to the mirror. "You're too adorable for words." She kissed the soft crook of his neck. "Mommy loves you."

"And Daddy loves Mommy."

She met Al's gaze in the mirror. He stood in the bedroom doorway, smiling at them.

"Are you ready?"

"I think so." She turned. "The diaper bag is packed, and their blankets are already in the car, in case it turns cold while we're out."

Al walked toward her. "Here. Let me have Wes, and you can get Sunni." As he took the baby from her arms, he leaned forward and kissed her on the cheek. "You look pretty tonight."

Her cheeks grew warm. Silly to blush at a compliment from her husband, but the words were so nice to hear. "Thanks."

"I'm glad we're doing this."

"Me too."

"Let's go."

With a nod, she turned toward the pink bassinet and lifted Sunni into her arms. Her daughter was all smiles. Patti hoped she would stay that way for a few hours.

Twenty minutes later, they pulled into Jeff Cavanaugh's driveway. Before they had the babies out of their car seats, their friend was waiting for them on the sidewalk.

"Good to see you two." Jeff came around the minivan to stand near Patti. "Can I help with anything?"

"If you wouldn't mind, there's a large diaper bag and a couple of blankets in the back. Could you get them for me?"

"Glad to." He moved to comply.

Al asked, "Who else did you invite over tonight?"

"Your brother and his girlfriend. A couple more of Penny's teacher friends. And you two. That makes eight adults. Pretty much packs my living room." He slapped Al on the back. "Come on. You're the last to arrive. Everybody's in the kitchen, eating snacks. We'd better join them before the food's gone."

"If my brother's in there, it's probably gone already."

Patti laughed as she headed up the sidewalk. Her husband spoke only half in jest. Eric Bedford, five years younger than Al, was tall, thin, and always hungry.

They were barely in the door before Penny and the three other women gathered around the babies. In moments, both Sunni and Weston were out of their carriers, *oohed* and *aahed* over, and passed from one set of arms to another.

ROBIN LEE HATCHER

Penny touched Patti's shoulder. "Patti, you know Susan."

She smiled at Eric's girlfriend. "Good to see you."

"You too."

"And you know Cassandra and Rene."

"How are you, Cassandra? Hi, Rene."

Rene Brewster had been in the same grade in school with Patti, although they were never close friends. Married at eighteen and divorced before she was twenty-five, Rene was plain and plump, her smiles never quite touching the perpetual melancholy in her dark eyes.

In contrast, the never-married Cassandra Coble, daughter of the town's police chief, sparkled with laughter. Whenever Patti saw her, she was struck by the younger woman's stunning beauty. She'd wondered more than once why Cassandra chose teaching in Hart's Crossing instead of modeling or acting or some other glamorous profession. She was certain Cassandra could have written her own ticket in Los Angeles or New York.

"Hey, Sis!"

Patti barely had time to turn before she found herself embraced by her brother-in-law.

"Man, you've gotten skinny." He gave her a peck on the cheek.

"Hardly." She kissed him back. "And you won't stay skinny if you keep eating everything in sight."

He feigned offense. "Where's that nephew of mine? He won't insult me."

"Good luck getting him away from Susan."

*It's good to see Patti enjoying herself*, Al thought as he watched from the opposite side of the kitchen island. His wife hadn't looked this carefree since before the twins were born.

How much of that was his fault?

Things had been better between them this past week. They hadn't fought once, and he was grateful. He didn't like to argue with his wife. He wanted to make her happy, and he seemed to fail at that too often. Half the time he didn't know what he did to start their disagreements, but he did seem to be responsible the majority of the time.

"Troubles, Al?" Cassandra stepped to his side.

"No." He shook his head. "I was thinking it's been a while since Patti and I got together with friends like this."

"Well, I imagine being the parents of twins keeps you more than a little busy."

"Yeah." He looked across the kitchen again, watching as Patti placed Weston in Eric's arms. "It can be crazy."

"But you love being a dad." Cassandra laid her hand lightly on his wrist. "I can see it in your eyes."

"Yeah, I love it."

"It's a big responsibility. A wife and kids, mortgage and a job." Her voice lowered. "I admire you, Al. You're a special guy."

His skin felt hot beneath her fingertips. The musky scent of her cologne filled his nostrils as she leaned closer.

"Your wife's a lucky girl."

Something dangerous coiled inside Al, an awareness of a woman who found him . . . interesting.

A slight smile curved the corners of Cassandra's mouth. Her eyebrows arched, as if she'd asked a question. Was she flirting with him? No. They were talking about his wife, for Pete's sake. He was imagining things—and not the sort of things he should imagine.

"Hey, everyone," Jeff said in a loud voice. "Let's get started. The Balderdash game board's set up in the living room."

Cassandra's smile broadened. "This should be fun. I love word games."

Al watched her walk away, then turned to look at Patti. But his wife's back was toward him as she, too, followed Jeff into the living room.

Some things a wife knew. No one had to tell her. She just knew. Like that instant her husband noticed Cassandra in a new way.

The joy went out of Patti's evening, right then and there.

Within a half hour of the start of the first game,

she had to step out of the room so she could nurse Sunni. Seated in the eating nook, she listened to the sudden bouts of laughter coming from the living room. She swore she could pick out the exact lilt of Cassandra's laugh mixing with Al's deeper one.

The room turned cold. Her breath felt labored.

Was she jealous? She needn't be. Al might notice a beautiful woman like Cassandra, but he wouldn't stray. He loved her.

So why did she feel alone and rejected? And afraid.

She thought of the extra weight clinging to her hips and thighs, of the loose skin on her belly that hadn't yet snapped back to its previous firmness. Would it ever? Did it bother Al that she wasn't as lithe as when they first married? He never said so. He told her she was beautiful. But was that true? Or was it something he thought he needed to say?

Tears pooled in her eyes, and a lump formed in her throat.

*"And Daddy loves Mommy."*

The memory of his words soothed her a little.

Cassandra was Al's colleague. Nothing more. She had nothing to fear.

Did she?

No, of course not. She was letting her hormones run away with her emotions again.

After Sunni was fed and burped, Patti placed the baby in her infant seat and returned to the living room just as Al was declared the winner.

Jeff said, "I never knew you were such a good liar, Bedford."

"Liar? Please. It was pure skill, my friend. I'm adept at language arts."

"Yeah. Sure."

Cassandra leaned forward and plucked her game piece off the board, then moved it back to the starting point. "I was only three spots behind. Next time I'll win."

"Not if I can keep you from it." Penny looked at Jeff. "Is there a kid's version of this game?"

He shrugged. "Don't know."

"It might be a fun way to teach word definitions. Especially for older kids." Penny turned toward Al. "Maybe the winner could get special privileges on that combined field trip for the fifth and sixth graders."

Cassandra clapped her hands together. "Oh, I have something even better. We could pit my fifth graders against Al's six graders. My students would love it. And we'd win too."

"Hey"—Al feigned insult—"you're forgetting that the sixth-grade teacher . . . that would be me . . . already beat the fifth-grade teacher." He grinned. "That would be you."

"He's got you there, Cassandra," Jeff said.

Patti listened to the good-natured banter and felt herself shriveling on the inside. Left out. Excluded.

Did Al even remember she was there?

It was nearly midnight by the time Al drove the minivan into the garage and cut the engine. "I'm glad you accepted Jeff's invitation. It was fun."

"Yes," Patti replied softly as she opened the passenger-side door.

He got out, too, and went around the car to help her with the babies, both of them sound asleep. "Didn't you have fun?"

"It was alright." She headed into the house, diaper bag on one shoulder, Sunni's infant carrier gripped with two hands.

He followed with Weston. "Did something happen to upset you?"

"No."

"Something's wrong."

"Nothing's wrong." Her tone held an edge of warning.

"You're sure?"

"I'm sure."

He frowned. She wasn't telling the truth. Something was wrong. She'd enjoyed herself when they first got to Jeff's, but then she'd suddenly stopped participating. The twins hadn't been a lot of trouble. Not enough to keep her from playing the game with the others.

As they put the babies to bed, Al's thoughts replayed the events of the evening. For the life of him, he couldn't figure out what had spoiled things for

Patti. She'd been all smiles for a while. Had someone said something to hurt her feelings? If so, he didn't know what.

He went downstairs to turn off the lights and check the locks, stopping long enough in the kitchen to put a couple of glasses into the dishwasher. When he looked up, Patti was watching him from the doorway.

"Al?" Her voice was soft and sad. "Why don't you tell me about what's happening at school? I didn't know any of the things you and the others talked about tonight. Jeff knows more from Penny than I do from you, and he's just her boyfriend."

He straightened. "What should I have told you?"

"Well, what about the field trip you're planning for the fifth and sixth graders?"

He had the feeling he should understand more than she had said. "We haven't firmed anything up yet. What's to tell?"

"Jeff knew." Tears slipped down her cheeks.

Why was she crying? Over a field trip?

"Penny isn't even involved, but she told Jeff about it."

Weariness washed over Al. He was tired of doing or saying the wrong thing all the time. Why couldn't something go right between them? Why couldn't Patti sustain a good mood for longer than five minutes?

Swallowing a sigh, he said, "Honey, I'm sorry. I didn't know you wanted me to tell you everything about my workday. But if that's what you want, I'll tell you." He stepped around the kitchen island and pulled her into his arms. "I promise."

# CHAPTER SIX

Al went to church alone the next morning. Patti said she was too tired to go. She and the twins would stay home.

To be honest, it was a relief. No minivan. No diaper bags. No infant carriers. No temperamental wife who was either angry or in tears.

*Great attitude for a Sunday.*

But who could blame him? He felt as if he were trapped in a pinball machine, never knowing what was going to bang into him next. *Boing! Boing! Boing!* One minute Patti was in a good mood, and the next she was mad or crying. Or both.

Arriving late, he slipped into the empty back

row and joined with the singing in progress, but his worship wasn't heartfelt. He didn't get lost in the lyrics and music, not like he did most Sundays. His thoughts kept drifting to Patti. He kept wondering what he was doing wrong, why they weren't as happy as they used to be.

She was unhappy too often.

He was unhappy too often.

*God, what's wrong with us?*

The music ended, and the people in the row in front of him turned to say good morning and shake his hand. He pasted on a smile, pretending all was well.

*Hypocrite.*

Patti carried the box from Sweet Baby Things into the nursery. Two matching cribs were placed against opposite walls, two matching dressers beside them, the drawers packed with baby clothes. The way the twins were growing, they would soon be sleeping here rather than in their bassinets in the master bedroom.

Kneeling on the floor beneath the large window, she cut the packing tape on the box and opened the lid to look at her latest purchase. Al wouldn't be happy when he saw the price tag.

But how could he complain? She needed this. Wasn't he always telling her they had to cut the *wants* and buy the *needs*? Well, this was a need. Even he would have to see that.

Except she should have discussed it with him before placing the order. Over three hundred dollars? How could she spend that kind of money without checking with him first? But hadn't he said he didn't want her to use formula? So wasn't this the next logical step?

Her stomach churned as she imagined their raised voices. She sat on the floor, leaned her back against the wall, and closed her eyes.

*I don't want to fight anymore. I don't want to be a nag.*

A nagging wife was as annoying as the constant dripping on a rainy day. That's what Proverbs said. That's what she'd become to Al. A constant dripping. A spendthrift who spent three hundred dollars in the middle of the night.

The image of the carefree Cassandra popped into her head, and she felt sick to her stomach. Sick with dread. Cassandra liked Al, maybe a little too much. Cassandra was gorgeous, thin, and employed in the same profession that Al loved with his whole heart.

There wasn't anything interesting about Patti. Not anymore. When she and Al were dating, she often talked to him about various manuscripts as she shepherded them through the publishing process. She would sing the praises of some wonderful new author. Sometimes she would ask him, as a man, would he read a story about this or that?

Nowadays, her conversations were about babies and diapers and housework and how tired she was. Some days she felt lucky to make it into the shower. She spent money she shouldn't, lost her temper too easily, and cried over nothing.

Speaking of tears . . .

She grabbed a cloth diaper from the stack on the nearby changing table and dried her eyes. Then she allowed her gaze to sweep the nursery, remembering when she and Al painted the room a few months before the twins were born.

It had been a warm Saturday in early May, warm enough to open the windows while they worked. Al had stood on the stepladder, carefully applying the sky blue paint on the wall near the ceiling, while Patti worked with equal care around the white window casing. They'd been at it about an hour when she paused to stretch. Her back ached, and she felt starved for air. Sometimes she would swear one of these babies slept on top of her lungs. A tiny moan escaped her lips as she released a deep breath of air.

Al was down the ladder in an instant. "You okay?" he asked, his face wreathed in concern. "Maybe you should go sit down."

"Don't be silly. I just needed to stretch. I'm all right."

"I should have asked Eric to help. You shouldn't be around these fumes."

She set the brush on the edge of the paint can, then with hands on his shoulders, pulled him forward for a kiss, her distended belly trying its best to keep them apart. "Stop worrying. The window's open. There's plenty of fresh air."

She started to draw away. He pulled her close again.

"I like those flecks of blue in your hair. Did I tell you that?" Laughter filled his eyes.

"I've got paint in my hair?"

He nodded. "I like it. Goes with the paint on your nose."

"I don't have paint on my nose."

He took his right thumb and drew it across the tip of her nose, then held it up for her to see. Sure enough, there was a smudge of blue paint on it. His smile broadened as he watched her.

In a flash of insight, she guessed the truth. "The paint was on your thumb. You just put it on my nose. Why you—" She clasped his head between her hands and pulled him downward, as if for a kiss. But at the last moment, she turned and rubbed the end of her nose against his, Eskimo-style. "Ha! Got you back."

"Mrs. Bedford, you're in serious trouble now." He swept her off her feet and into his arms, carrying her out of the nursery and into their bedroom while he peppered her with kisses and spread the blue paint around.

Oh, that had been a happy day. Just one of many happy days as they painted and decorated this room and dreamed of what it would be like when the babies arrived.

It hadn't been so very long ago. Only a matter of months. Could they be happy like that again?

*Please, God. Let us be happy like that again.*

The sermon that morning was on stewardship, and Al felt God trying to tell him something through the pastor's words. He had an awful feeling that he wasn't doing much of a job of managing God's blessings.

He shouldn't have let Patti talk him into buying their house. It was too much for them with only one salary. And it wasn't just the mortgage. It was the heat and electricity and water and sewer too. And the insurance.

But what could he do about all of that now? Sell the house? Patti would be heartbroken. Wasn't she sad enough already?

73

With those glum thoughts roiling in his head, Al arrived at the side exit of the church at the same time as Till Hart.

"Good morning, Al." The elderly woman—in her midseventies but as spry as many who were more than a decade younger—smiled at him. "Where's that pretty wife of yours? Not to mention those precious babies."

"They stayed home this morning, Miss Hart. Patti was feeling a bit run-down and wanted to rest."

"Oh? I hope she isn't catching that bug that's been going around. Francine Hunter was sick last week and has been coughing up a storm ever since. Tell Patti I'll pray for her."

*Pray for us both. We need it.* "I will."

Her brows drew together. "You look a little peaked yourself. Are you all right?"

"Yes," he lied. "I'm fine." He pushed open the glass door and motioned her through.

"Well, all right then." She didn't sound convinced. "Be sure to tell Patti that she can call on me if she needs a hand with the little ones. I'm a good baby-sitter."

"Thanks, Miss Hart. I'll tell her."

They said their farewells on the sidewalk before turning in different directions, Al headed for the parking lot, Till Hart walking home as she always did in nice weather.

He made it to his car without running into others who might want to pass the time of day. Thankful for that—not wanting to feel more of a hypocrite than he already did—he slipped into the red Spider, then sat there, hands on the steering wheel, not wanting to go home yet, not sure what he would say to Patti when he got there.

Maybe a drive would help clear his head.

He started the engine, left the parking lot, and followed the road out of Hart's Crossing, picking up speed as he reached the main highway. The wind felt good in his hair, and for a time, he thought of nothing except the way the sports car hugged the road. But eventually, he remembered why he took the drive in the first place. To figure things out. To figure Patti out.

He'd driven several miles into the mountains by the time he slowed the car and turned off the road at a lookout point. He parked near the Idaho highway historical marker and got out, walking to the metal railing that overlooked the valley.

*Figure out Patti.*

Was that even possible? Could a man really understand a woman? He used to think he could, but lately . . .

He thought back to their honeymoon. They had planned their wedding to coincide with the beginning of spring break and had left the next day for a week in Hawaii. Each night, they took long walks on the beach, holding hands, sharing their hopes and dreams for the future. Even when they said nothing, it seemed they were in communion with each other.

When had that stopped? When had he stopped knowing what she wanted before she asked? It seemed to him it was about the same time that he started waking up in the middle of the night, wondering how he could make his paycheck stretch another week, wondering if their credit was going to end up in ruins. Or worse. He tried to make Patti understand without letting her know how worried he was. He tried, but he wasn't doing a good job of it. They never talked about money these days. They fought over it.

How could he make things better? They never should have bought that house. Not after Patti lost her editing job. Not when they were about to start a family with two babies at once. Oh, their finances looked tight but okay on paper. But most of the time, he felt like he couldn't breathe when his thoughts turned to money.

He shook his head, a rueful smile touching his lips. He'd come up here to think about Patti, and where were his thoughts? Back on their finances instead. Only maybe the two were tied together.

He loved his wife. He wanted her to be happy all the time, not just now and then. He wanted her to laugh the way she used to. He wanted her to look at him with trust, with eyes that said, "I know you'll never hurt or disappoint me."

*How do I make that happen, God? How?*

A twin in each arm, Patti glanced at the mantel clock in the living room, turned, and walked back to the kitchen. The clock on the stove said the same thing: 1:37.

Where was Al? He should have been home more than an hour ago.

She paced to the living room window and stared out at the street.

This wasn't like him, not to come home, not to call if delayed. Even when he was angry with her, he wasn't the thoughtless sort. He was dependable, the type of man who did what he said he would do, who checked his day planner so he never missed an appointment, and who kept the budget in a spreadsheet so the bills were paid on time. She liked those qualities about him. He made her feel safe.

Her own father had none of those qualities. Soon after he left her mother, her dad had moved away from Hart's Crossing. Phone calls dwindled from once a month to once a year to an occasional birthday or Christmas. He didn't make it to Patti and Al's wedding.

Weston started to fuss, an outward expression of his mother's inward feelings. With a soft moan, she turned from the window and carried the babies toward the stairs. Her right foot was on the bottom step when she heard the garage door open. She turned toward the kitchen. A moment later, Al came into view.

*Where were you? Why didn't you call me?*

"Sorry I didn't come straight home. I . . . I went for a drive. I needed time to think."

She pictured Cassandra placing her fingers against Al's wrist. "What about?" Her heart raced. Maybe she didn't want to hear his answer.

"About why we fight so much when neither one of us wants to."

Her heart stopped racing. It hardly seemed to beat at all. "Did you figure it out?"

"Not yet, but I will."

She swallowed the lump that had formed in her throat. "I was taking the twins upstairs. Their diapers need to be changed, and Wes is getting hungry."

"Here." Al moved toward her. "I'll help you." He took Weston into his arms.

What should she say to him? Was it better to talk or be silent? She wasn't sure. She used to be sure about everything. Now nothing seemed certain.

In silence, she turned and ascended the stairs, Al following right behind. They entered the master bedroom, took identical changing mats, baby wipes, and disposable diapers from the small bureau near the bassinets, then placed the mats and babies on the floor and knelt beside them.

"Miss Hart asked about you after the service," Al said. "She said to call her if you need a babysitter."

Here it was. The golden opportunity to tell him about her extravagant purchase.

"Al, I . . ." She swallowed, searching for the words.

"Yeah?"

"Maybe we *can* use Miss Hart sometime. I . . . I've decided to give the babies a bottle every now and then. So I don't have to be with them for every feeding. Not formula, though."

*Tell him. Tell him the whole truth.*

She glanced up, and the words stuck in her throat. He looked as uncertain as she felt. He didn't want to fight, and neither did she.

Tomorrow would be soon enough. She would tell him tomorrow.

# CHAPTER SEVEN

Somehow, one day became two, which became three, which became more, and still Patti didn't tell Al about the charge on the credit card. Why make waves when they were getting along?

But her reprieve couldn't last forever. The credit card bill would arrive one of these days. Delaying would only make things worse. Unless she could get a little help. And there was only one person she could ask.

Early on Friday morning, she picked up the phone and dialed, punching in the extension when asked for it.

"Janet Alexander."

"Hi, Mom."

"Patti?"

"Sorry to call you at work."

"That's all right, dear. Let me close my office door." There was the sound of movement from the other end of the line. "There. Now tell me. What's up?"

"Nothing much. You know how it is in Hart's Crossing. One day's pretty much like another. The twins are growing like weeds, and Al and I are both well even though there's a virus or the flu or something going around since school started."

"Are you getting more rest?"

"Yes. The twins are sleeping longer stretches at night. Not all the way through but almost."

"Good. That's always a relief."

Patti chewed her lower lip for a moment. "Mom . . . you know how you told me that I needed to get out more? You know, have a breather from the babies, see a movie, go to the diner."

"Of course I remember."

"I haven't been able to yet, but I decided to start feeding the babies sometimes from a bottle so they'll get used to it. Then we can hire a sitter, and Al and I can go out together. Only we're both against the idea of using formula." Her words came faster. "Anyway, I was looking around online, and I found this breast pump that all the mothers rave about, so I ordered it. It's absolutely the perfect thing. It's making a huge difference. Only"—she drew a quick breath—"I need a little help with the cost of it."

"How much?"

Her voice lowered. "Three hundred dollars."

"Three hundred dollars? My gracious, Patricia Ann. It must be made of pure gold."

"No." She choked on a sob. "It isn't."

"Patti? What's wrong?"

"Nothing." Her voice dropped to a whisper. "Everything."

"Take a deep breath, honey."

Patti wiped at the tears rolling down her cheeks. "I'm so tired of crying, Mom. I feel like such a baby. I'm trying to make a nice home for Al and the twins. I love them so much. But it seems like I can't do anything right. Al and I have been fighting a lot. Mostly about money."

Her mother was silent for a while before saying, "Did you argue about the three hundred dollars?"

"Not yet."

"You haven't told him you bought it?"

"No."

"Oh, honey. Keeping secrets isn't good for a marriage."

Patti stared out the window at the backyard. "I know. And it won't be a secret for long, because the credit card statement is about due." She sucked in a breath and let it out. "Will you help me, Mom? If you lend me the money, I'll pay you back a little each month."

She hated the silence that followed. She could imagine the wheels turning in her mom's head as she debated the pros and cons of bailing Patti out of trouble. The amount of money wouldn't bother her mother. Janet and Doug Alexander lived comfortable lives, and both made good incomes in their respective careers. Her mom's concern would be whether or not giving Patti the money was the right thing to do, the best thing to do. She was probably praying about it while Patti waited, holding her breath.

At last, the silence ended.

"I'll give you the money, dear, on one condition. Actually, several conditions. First, you tell Al what you did. No more secrets. The two of you need to have a serious conversation about your finances and then live within the boundaries. Second, if you two are fighting as much as you say you are, you need to consider counseling. Two people can love each other and still need help learning to communicate. There is no shame in that. And third, tell your doctor how you're feeling. Maybe the problem is more than lack of sleep or a need to get out of the house a bit more."

Patti didn't protest the conditions her mom set. She had no right to protest. Besides, it was good advice. Even in her emotional state she recognized that. "Okay."

"I'll put the check in the mail today."

"Thanks, Mom. I really appreciate it. Really."

"I know, dear. I love you very much. You take care of yourself, and give my love to Al and the babies."

"I will. I love you too. Bye."

"Good-bye."

With a sigh, Patti returned the handset to the charger, her thoughts racing ahead to that evening and the promised conversation with her husband.

Al stood on the spot where blacktop met school-yard and watched the kids at play during their lunch break. Laughter and shouts abounded. There was a group climbing on the playground equipment, others kicking around a soccer ball, a few taking swings at a baseball with a bat, some sitting in bunches on the grass. No injuries. No fighting. That was just the way he wanted it when he was assigned playground duty.

"Look out!"

He turned at the same moment the baseball went zipping past his head. He took a quick step backward. Not that it mattered. By that time, the ball was past him and bouncing across the blacktop.

Lyssa Sampson jogged toward him. "Sorry, Mr. Bedford. You okay?"

"Yeah." He touched his temple, as if checking to see if he'd been hit. "Better watch those wild pitches."

"I didn't throw it." She jerked a thumb behind her. "It was a foul ball. Blame Vince. He hit it."

As if he'd heard what Lyssa said, Vince Johnson shouted, "Sorry, Mr. Bedford."

Al waved at the boy to let him know all was well.

Lyssa hurried after the baseball, obviously eager to return to the game.

Al chuckled. Moments like this, there was no doubt in his heart that he was born to be a teacher. He loved working with kids, shaping young minds, challenging them to achieve great things. He had to love it. Nobody entered public education—especially in a small school district—because they wanted to get rich.

*Rich isn't necessary, but more would be nice.*

The thought brought a frown to his brow. He hated that money—or the lack thereof—was constantly on his mind. It made him feel petty and complaining. As a Christian, shouldn't he have an attitude of gratitude instead? Shouldn't his first thoughts be about how much God had blessed him?

He turned, preparing to walk to the opposite end of the schoolyard. That's when he saw Cassandra heading toward him. She was smiling, and there was a jaunty spring in her step that made her seem not a whole lot older than some of the kids on the playground.

"Did you hear?" she asked as she drew near.

"Hear what?"

"Our field trip to the Craters of the Moon is a definite go."

"That's great."

"I know. I can think of at least a dozen projects my class can work on in relation to it."

Cassandra's excitement was palpable. Would she one day find herself worried about paying the mortgage and car payment and grocery bill from her teacher's salary?

"Al . . . What's troubling you?"

It bothered him that she could read him so well. It felt . . . wrong. Why was that?

He shook his head. "Nothing."

"If you ever need to talk, you know I'm only a classroom away."

"Sure. Thanks." He was saved from saying more

by the ringing of the school bell calling kids back to class.

Gretchen Livingston, an attractive woman in her midthirties, took a sip of vanilla chai tea and smiled. "Patti, this is so good. Thanks for making me a cup."

"I'm glad you like it."

Patti's neighbor ran her fingers through her short blonde hair. "Oh, my. It's good to have a weekday off. It's so much easier to accomplish things around the house when I'm the only one at home."

"Sometimes I don't think I'll catch up until the twins are in high school."

Gretchen laughed. "I remember feeling that way when Amy was a baby. I can only imagine what it's like for you."

"Speaking of Amy"—Patti sat down opposite Gretchen and motioned with her head toward the family room where Amy sat with the twins—"she's been such a help to me."

"Well, don't let her become a pest. You send her home anytime you don't want her here."

"She's never a pest, believe me. I hope my two will be as well-mannered when they're thirteen."

Gretchen smiled again. "That's a great compliment. Thanks."

"It's just the truth." Patti lowered her gaze to the cup on the table. "Gretchen, when Amy was a newborn, were you ever . . . did you ever—" She stopped and drew in a deep breath. "I'm so moody lately. Mom thinks maybe I should see a counselor. She wonders if I might have postpartum depression or something." As soon as she said it, she was sorry. She liked Gretchen and all, but they weren't close friends. Did she want her neighbors knowing her deep dark secrets? No!

Gretchen gave her shoulders a slight shrug as she shook her head. "I didn't get depressed after Amy was born, but I was really tired, so everything seemed twice as hard as it really was." She took another sip of tea. "But if you decide you need a counselor, I can recommend someone to you. Hayley Young. Do you know her?"

Patti shook her head.

"She has an office on Idaho south of Main Street. Very soft-spoken and gentle. I went to see her a couple of years ago for a few months when I was struggling with something. She was a great help to me."

Gretchen couldn't know it, but just hearing she'd sought the help of a counselor herself made Patti feel less of a failure as a wife and mom. And as a woman.

"Now, I'd better get home so I can accomplish a few more of those nagging to-do items." Gretchen finished the last of her tea, then rose and carried her cup to the kitchen sink. As she headed for the back door, she called, "Amy, don't forget Mrs. Hargrove is picking you up at five o'clock."

"I won't, Mom. See you in a while."

Patti followed Gretchen to the door. "Thanks for coming over. And for telling me about Hayley Young."

"Glad to help, Patti. Have a nice evening."

"We will."

As she closed the back door, she breathed a silent prayer. *Please, let it be a nice evening.*

# CHAPTER EIGHT

Delicious odors greeted Al as he entered the kitchen. Patti stood at the counter, holding the lid of the electric frying pan in one hand and a large pronged fork in the other.

"Smells good." It was one of his favorite meals, a juicy roast cooked with onions, carrots, and potatoes. When they were first married, Patti had asked his mother to show her how to prepare the dinner the way he liked it.

She turned her head and smiled. "Hi, honey. I didn't hear the garage door." She set the lid on the pan. "Dinner should be ready soon."

"The twins asleep?" He stepped forward and kissed her on the lips.

"Mmm."

He drew back. "Does that mean yes or no?"

She cocked her head toward the family room. "Have a look."

Lately, he and Patti had been so careful what they said and how they said it. It was exhausting. A little like the proverbial walking on eggshells. But their methods seemed to be working.

He moved toward the family room. There, seated in the rocking chair, was Amy Livingston, Sunni in the crook of one arm, a bottle of milk in her opposite hand. Weston lay on a blanket on the floor, staring at a portable mobile.

"Amy came over after school again." Patti stepped to his side. "She already fed Wes, and now she's taking care of Sunni. I never would have gotten dinner ready on time without her help."

The girl glanced over her shoulder. "Hi, Mr. Bedford."

"Hey, Amy."

Patti touched his arm. "They've taken to the bottles of breast milk without complaint." Her voice lowered. "I thought maybe we could ask Amy and Miss Hart to watch the babies for a few hours next weekend or the one after so you and I could go out to eat and maybe see a movie."

"Amy *and* Miss Hart?"

"Yes. I'm afraid the twins would be too much for Miss Hart alone. She is seventy-six, after all. Amy's a great help, but she's still kind of young to be in charge. So I thought the two of them . . ." She let the explanation drift into silence, unfinished.

He cupped the side of her face with his right hand. "Sounds like a good idea to me. I'll check the *Press* and see what's playing at the Apollo."

The local weekly paper, the *Mountain View Press*, listed movie schedules for four weeks out. Although the Apollo Theater—which showed movies Friday through Sunday—rarely got first-run movies, most of the good films found their way to Hart's Crossing eventually. There should be something worth seeing in the next couple of weeks.

Patti's smile made her brown eyes sparkle. "Great."

She kissed him on the cheek. "I'd better check on the roast. I don't want it to dry out."

Al watched her go, then entered the family room and lifted his son into his arms. "Amy, would you like to ask your mom if you can stay for dinner? I'm sure there's plenty."

"No, thanks. I'm gonna spend the night at a friend's house. I'll have to leave pretty soon." She set the empty bottle aside and lifted Sunni to her cloth-covered shoulder, softly patting her back.

"You're getting to be a pro at that."

"Thanks. I took a child-care class at the school this summer. I like helping Mrs. Bedford with the babies. They're sweet." She laughed. "Most of the time."

Al chuckled as he settled onto the sofa. "Most of the time." He pressed his nose into the curve of Weston's shoulder and breathed in the baby softness. It was like a breath of joy, a reminder of how blessed he was, and how often he let the cares of the world make him forget it.

*Thank you, Father, for trusting me with this family.*

"Mr. Bedford?"

He opened his eyes to find Amy standing near the sofa.

"Do you want to hold Sunni too, or should I put her on the blanket? I gotta go now."

"I'll take her, Amy. Thanks."

The girl placed Sunni in the crook of Al's free arm, the two babies forming a *V* against his chest. "Did Mrs. Bedford tell you I'm writing for the school newspaper this year?"

"No, she didn't."

"She's helping me with some of my stories. You know. With the grammar and stuff. I'm thinking maybe someday I'll write a book and Mrs. Bedford could be my editor. Wouldn't that be cool?"

"Sure would."

She gave him a half wave, turned on her heel, and left, calling to Patti as she passed through the kitchen, "See you later, Mrs. Bedford."

"Bye, Amy," Patti returned. "Thanks for everything."

Al glanced from one twin to the other and felt the joy of fatherhood well up in him again. "Either one of you planning to be a writer when you grow up?"

Weston blew bubbles from his mouth and wriggled in Al's arm.

"Guess that means no." He leaned his head against the back of the sofa. *I wonder what you will be.*

His thoughts drifted to scenes from his own childhood. Warm summer days spent playing ball with friends or camping out in his backyard with his younger brother. Picnics with his mom's famous fried chicken, baked beans, coleslaw, and corn on the cob. Helping his dad feed the livestock and the way hay got into his hair and clothes, making him itch. Learning to drive the old, beat-up, two-ton farm truck the summer he was twelve. Knowing just about everybody in town, neighbor helping neighbor. Strict but loving parents.

It was a good life that he remembered. He wanted his children to have a similar childhood—safe, happy, without want for anything they needed. He would do anything to make that happen.

"Al? Dinner's ready." Patti stepped into view. "Are they awake?"

"Sunni's getting a little drowsy. Wes is wide awake, but I don't think he'll fuss if I put him down."

"Maybe they'll sleep while we eat."

"Hope so."

He rose from the sofa and carried the babies to the large blanket spread on the family room carpet, knelt, and laid them down. He waited to see if either would protest. They didn't.

After washing his hands in the kitchen sink, he went to the table, where Patti stood beside her chair, waiting for him. He kissed her cheek. "Everything looks great."

She gave him a tentative smile. "Sit down before it gets cold."

Something about her manner had changed since he first got home. She seemed nervous or tense. He decided not to say anything, though. Better not to make waves. He could tell she was trying hard to please him. He didn't want to upset her by saying the wrong thing.

He held the back of her chair while she sat. Then he took his own place. He reached for her hand and bowed his head, and together they thanked God for all he provided.

Several times during the meal, Al said how good it was, but Patti tasted little of what she put in her mouth. Her stomach was tied in too many knots to enjoy the dinner she'd labored over.

When should she tell him? When was the right time? While they were still eating? Or should she wait until they relaxed on the sofa? Maybe after a little television. Was one of his favorite shows on tonight? Perhaps she should let him watch it first.

No. She needed to do it now. She'd waited long enough. Another few minutes and she would explode from the tension she felt inside.

"Al." She set her fork on her plate. "I need to tell you something."

"What's that?"

*Just say it. Just get it out and over with.* "There's going to be a charge on the next credit card bill. It's from a store called Sweet Baby Things. The amount's pretty big, but I don't want you to be upset when you see it." She folded her hands in her lap, trying to hide her nerves. "My mom's paying for it. She's already sent the check. So you don't have to worry about it."

"What did you buy?"

"Remember when we had that discussion about adding formula to the twins' diet? Well, I decided you were right, that we didn't want to do that. Mom thinks it would do us both good to get out, but we need babysitters, and the babysitters need to be able to feed the babies if they get hungry. So that's when I placed the order."

She was prevaricating, telling the truth and yet not quite. Why should it matter, she asked herself, that these things happened in a slightly different order?

"I still don't know what you bought," Al said.

She told him about the pump, explaining why it was absolutely top of the line and how terrific it was and why it would make her life as a nursing mother of twins so much easier. "It's what I used for those bottles Amy was feeding the babies when you got home." She couldn't tell from his expression what he was thinking.

"How much did it cost, Patti?"

"Three hundred and twenty dollars."

He echoed her in a soft voice. "Three hundred and twenty dollars. That's a lot."

"Mom's paying for it. Well, most of it. Three hundred is what she sent."

"She shouldn't have to pay for any of it." He placed his napkin on the table beside the plate and rose from his chair. With three strides, he arrived at the window, his hands shoved into the pockets of his trousers. "I should be able to buy the things you need."

Guilt twisted her insides.

"I should provide for my family."

"You *do* provide for us."

"Not well enough." He turned to face her, defeat in his eyes. "Maybe it's time I look for a position in a bigger school district. If I start now, I might have another job by the start of the next school year."

Strange, she'd nagged him about that very thing for a number of months. But when he said it, it sounded awful.

"We don't have to decide that tonight," she said.

She wanted to go to him, put her arms around him, hold him tight, and tell him she loved him. Guilt kept her from doing so.

102

# CHAPTER NINE

"Hey, hon." Al stood in the doorway to the garage, wiping greasy hands on a rag. "When I'm done changing the oil in the cars, how about we drive out to the farm."

Patti looked at her husband. The distance between them felt much farther than the width of the kitchen. "Sure. If you'd like."

"My folks haven't seen the twins in a week or so."

"I know. Your mom's got that charity event coming up soon, and your dad's getting ready for harvest."

They were talking but saying nothing that needed

to be said. It was like being in a line dance and not knowing the steps, afraid to move, afraid to stand still.

He nodded. "Okay then. I'll give them a call and tell them we're coming after lunch." He looked as if he might say something more, then turned and stepped out of sight.

Seconds later, Patti heard the garage door close. The sound made her chest hurt. She went into the living room and sat on the sofa, closing her eyes, letting the temporary silence of the house envelop her.

She wanted things to be right between her and Al. She wanted things to be the way they used to be. She wanted to tell him all of her thoughts and feelings without hesitation. But how could she make that happen?

*Perhaps with God's help?*

She smiled sadly. She was no better at being honest with God than she was with Al. When was the last time she prayed, really prayed? When was the last time she tried to hear his voice?

Months. Many months. Long before she could blame it on the busyness of motherhood.

"I've made such a mess of things, Father. I've hurt Al, and I don't know how to undo the things I've done. Can you help me find my way? I don't even know how to start."

Al's great-grandfather had moved to south-central Idaho in 1915, soon after a canal system brought irrigation to the area. He started with 160 acres, and as his circumstances improved, he acquired more land, as did his son and his grandson, Al's dad. The Bedford farm today was nearly a thousand acres of apple orchards, corn fields, and row upon row of onions.

Within moments of Al bringing the minivan to a stop in front of the house, his mom appeared on the porch. "We're so glad you came," she called as she descended the steps.

Al got out of the van and hugged his mom. "Hope we're not intruding."

"Don't be silly. Seeing you and your family is the best part of any day." She kissed his cheek. "Now, let's get those babies into the house before they catch a chill."

"A chill? It's seventy-five degrees out."

She batted at his shoulder. "Don't argue with your mother."

"Yes, ma'am," he said with a laugh.

His mom rounded the minivan and hugged Patti. "How are you, dear?"

"I'm fine, Carolyne. Thanks."

"What can I do to help you?"

"If you'll carry Wes inside, I can handle Sunni and the diaper bag."

Al knew better than to get between grandmother and grandchildren. "Where's Dad?"

"Behind the barn. He's working on that old tractor he found at the auction last week."

"I'll see if I can give him a hand. Looks like you've got things under control here."

"Tell him there's pie when the two of you are ready to come in."

"What kind?"

"Strawberry rhubarb."

"Mmm." Nobody made a better pie than his mom,

and strawberry rhubarb was his favorite. "I think I'll tell him to hurry." He waited a moment, watching as the two women removed the infant seats from the backseat of the minivan. Then, seeing they wouldn't need his help, he strode toward the barn.

Mark Bedford farmed with modern equipment, but he had a penchant for antique tractors. He loved to buy, refurbish, and display them at the county fair. Tinkering with his collection brought him pleasure and relaxation.

Al found his dad lying on his back beneath a faded green John Deere. He stopped beside the large rear tire and leaned down. "Got yourself a new toy, I see."

"Hey, son. You here already? I thought I had another hour." His dad slid from under the tractor. "She's a beauty, isn't she? A 1953 Model 50. Runs pretty good. Won't take much to restore her." He stood and gave the machine an affectionate pat. "I got a good deal on her too."

"What does Mom think?"

His dad laughed. "Carolyne's just glad I've got a hobby that keeps me out from underfoot."

"But she might prefer model tractors to the real thing. They'd be cheaper and take up less space."

"True enough." He patted the antique tractor a second time before saying, "I imagine your mother's commandeered the grandkids. Suppose I ought to try to wrestle one of those babies away from her?"

"Not unless you want a broken arm. But she did say to tell you there's strawberry rhubarb pie ready for the eating."

"Well, what're we standing out here for?"

"My thoughts exactly."

"Help me put these tools away, will you?"

"Sure thing."

Within a matter of minutes, the tools were back in the toolbox and the toolbox was back in the barn. Then the two men started toward the house.

"Dad, I've been thinking about looking for a teaching position in one of the larger school districts. Maybe over in Boise."

His dad stopped walking. "You're not serious."

"Afraid so." He turned to face his father.

"But why?"

Al sighed. "Money." He shrugged. "My paycheck

doesn't stretch far enough these days. Not with four of us."

"Do you need a loan? If you do, I can——"

"No, Dad. Thanks, but this is something I've got to work out for myself."

"When would you move?"

"Probably not until the next school year. I'll have to send out resumes. See what's out there. I guess it could be sooner than next fall, if a position opened up somewhere midterm, but that's not likely."

His dad raked his fingers through graying hair. "It'll break your mother's heart if you move away. Especially now that she's got grandchildren."

"Let's not say anything to her for now. It hasn't happened yet. It's just something I'm thinking about."

And the thinking weighed heavy on his heart.

Standing at the open back door, Patti observed her husband and father-in-law as they talked outside the large weathered barn. After a few moments, Mark placed a hand on Al's right shoulder. A gesture of comfort? Of sympathy?

Tears stung her eyes.

Al was unhappy, and it was her fault. She'd nagged at him. She'd lied to him. Worst of all, she'd made him feel like a failure as a husband and provider. What if she'd gone too far? What if he fell out of love with her?

"Is something wrong, Patti?"

Her mother-in-law's gentle voice drew her around. She opened her mouth to say nothing was wrong, but instead said, "Do you remember my dad?"

"Yes, I remember Grant. I never knew him well, of course. We didn't move in the same social circles."

"Do you think he ever loved my mom?"

Her mother-in-law rinsed the mixing bowl in her hand and set it in the dish drainer. Then she dried her hands on a towel before turning toward Patti. "That's a question you should ask your mother."

"She doesn't like to talk about him. Even after all these years. I remember how hurt she was when he left us. And then she got angry and stayed that way for a long time."

Carolyne leaned a hip against the counter, arms crossed over her chest. "What's this about, dear? Why are you asking about your dad?"

The unwelcome tears fell from Patti's eyes, tracing her cheeks. "Sometimes I think Al must be sorry he married me."

"Gracious. What a thing to say!"

"I've made him miserable lately."

Carolyne hurried to her side. "Come into the living room and sit down." With an arm around Patti's back, her mother-in-law steered her toward the sofa. "Now, tell me what's troubling you."

She wanted to comply. She wanted to pour out her heart, but doing so would feel like another betrayal of her husband. She'd done too much of that already. She'd hurt Al in too many ways.

"Patti"—Carolyne's voice was gentle and low—"are you afraid Al might do what your father did?"

There it was—her greatest fear, out in the open. What if he left her because of the things she'd said and done? What if he decided he couldn't live with her tears, her moods, her spending?

*What if I've made him so unhappy he turns to someone*

ROBIN LEE HATCHER

*else?* She drew a shallow breath. *Someone like Cassandra Coble.*

She closed her eyes, wanting to shut out the pain in her heart.

"Al is nothing like Grant Sinclair." Carolyne placed the palm of her hand against Patti's cheek. "He isn't the type to walk out on his family. He loves you, and he loves those two precious babies. He isn't going anywhere without the three of you. I can promise you that. No matter what the trouble is, he'll go through it with you."

Patti looked at her mother-in-law, hoping she was right, wanting desperately to believe it.

Carolyne gave her an encouraging smile. "Every marriage goes through rough patches. Living with another person, no matter how much you love them, can be hard at times. And when you throw young kids into the mix . . ." She rolled her eyes. "When we were newlyweds, Mark and I used to fight like cats and dogs."

"You did?"

"Gracious, yes. That man was as stubborn as the day is long, and I was every bit as bad. My, we could butt heads. We still do, every now and then. And over the silliest things too."

Patti couldn't imagine her in-laws speaking a cross word to each other.

"Our biggest problem in the early years of marriage was I thought he should know what I felt, and he thought I should be able to read his mind. I've never known a single couple that worked for. It takes words to communicate."

Footsteps announced the arrival of the men on the back porch.

Carolyne stood. "Why don't you go wash away those tears? Then you and I can get ourselves a piece of that pie before those two eat it all." She smiled again. "And Patti, put away those worries. It'll turn out right. You'll see."

Al slid the empty plate into the center of the table.

"Would you like another slice?" his mom asked.

"Better not. Two was more than I needed." He

pushed his chair back from the table and patted his stomach. "I should've stopped at one."

His dad rocked Weston on his thighs. "When you get to be my age, you'll have to stop. If I didn't limit myself, I'd weigh three hundred pounds by now."

Al smiled as he tried to picture an overweight Mark Bedford. Impossible to do. His father, now in his midfifties, still wore the same size trousers as when he graduated from college. Al knew this because his parents had renewed their wedding vows on their thirtieth anniversary, and his dad was able to wear the suit he was married in.

His gaze traveled around the table as he remembered the Saturday he brought Patti home to meet his parents for the first time. They'd been dating a couple of months, and he already knew that Patti was destined to be more than just another girlfriend. Even that early in their relationship, he wanted his family to know she was special to him. He remembered the way Patti laughed that day at his dad's jokes—even the lame ones—and raved over his mom's cooking.

More memories of other good times in this old farmhouse kitchen drifted into his mind. Christmases and Thanksgivings when his grandparents were still living. Birthday parties, both his and Eric's. The day he and Patti told his parents they were engaged. The day they announced they were expecting. Another day when they informed his folks they were having twins.

If he and Patti moved away from Hart's Crossing, would their kids have the same sort of rich memories as he had? How often would they get to see his parents? Would Wes have the opportunity to tinker with Grandpa Mark on some old tractor? Would Sunni learn to bake pies with Grandma Carolyne in this big old kitchen?

But maybe he was idealizing everything. Maybe they would make even better memories in a new home in a new town. Maybe if he wasn't so stressed over finances, he would be a better husband and dad.

*It's about more than money.*

He looked across the kitchen table at his wife, who was listening to something his mom said. Love surged in his chest, a feeling so strong it was almost painful. Had she any idea how much he loved her?

*"And you husbands,"* Paul said in Ephesians, *"must love your wives with the same love Christ showed the church."*

Had he loved her that much? When he replayed the events of the past couple of weeks in his mind, he had to answer no. Even when he finally agreed that he would look into finding a better paying position, he'd done it with reluctance and an attitude that told her this was all her fault.

Pride. He'd let pride get in his way of doing the right things, of saying the right things.

*God, I'm sorry. Show me how to make it up to her.*

Patti glanced across the table at her husband and found him watching her.

*I don't want us to leave Hart's Crossing. This is our home.*

She hoped her mother-in-law was wrong. She hoped Al could read her mind. At least this once.

*I'm sorry, Al.*

Somewhere in the New Testament, wives were instructed to respect their husbands. There hadn't been much respect going on when she was insisting on her own way, when she was buying things their budget couldn't handle, when she was asking for money from her mother behind his back. Or when she let fears surface, fears that he might one day walk out, the same way her father had. What sort of faith did that show? It didn't show faith. It said she didn't trust him. And perhaps he felt that lack of trust.

But she could change all that. She *must* change it. She needed to share her uncertainties and fears. She'd held back parts of herself from him since the day they met, and that was wrong of her. He was her husband. She needed to trust him with her full self, her full heart.

This morning, she'd told God she needed to know how to start setting things right. Well, now she had her answer. She would begin with trust. Trusting Al. Trusting God.

# CHAPTER TEN

After putting the twins to bed for the night, Patti went in search of her husband. She found him in the family room with his laptop open, his fingers tapping on the keys.

"Are you working?" she asked as she sat on the sofa nearby.

He looked up. "I'm updating my resume."

"You don't need to do that."

"Yes, I do. It may take some time to find a better-paying position, but I think my qualifications are—"

"Al, I don't want you to find another job. I don't want us to move away from Hart's Crossing."

"You don't?" He closed the laptop. "What changed your mind?"

"I love you, Al, but I haven't shown it the way that I should. I . . . I've made things, possessions"—she motioned toward the room around them—"this house, more important than they should be. I guess that's how I wanted you to prove your love for me. By providing all these things." She drew in a shuddery breath. "I was afraid, and the more afraid I was and the more we fought, the more wrong choices I made and the farther away you seemed."

Al set the laptop on the coffee table and reached for Patti's hand. "I'm not far away. I'm right here. I'll always be right here."

"I've been afraid that you wouldn't be. Always here with me, I mean."

"You have?"

"Yes."

"But—"

She reached up with her free hand and touched her index finger to his lips. "Let me finish."

He nodded, his gaze not leaving hers.

"My parents used to fight all the time before

my dad walked out on us. When you and I started fighting, it brought up all of those unhappy memories. And then when I saw Cassandra flirting with you . . ."

Al's eyes widened.

"I was afraid I might be driving you to her."

"Patti, I would never be unfaithful, and I don't have any interest in Cassandra Coble."

She lowered her eyes to their clasped hands. "I know. Deep down inside, I know. But fear isn't very rational, is it?" When he didn't answer, she looked up again. "I think we should call Betty Frazier and put the house on the market. We can find a home with a smaller mortgage that is more suited to us."

"But you love this house."

"For the wrong reasons." Tears flooded her eyes. "And besides, I love you more."

With a tug on her hand, he drew her from the sofa and onto his lap, holding her close, her face nestled in the curve of his neck and shoulder.

"I'm sorry, Al. I'm sorry for not being honest, for not trusting you, for making you feel as if you've failed me. You haven't."

"I'm sorry too." His breath brushed her ear as he spoke. "I could've done a lot of things differently. I love you, Patti."

She felt her body relax in his embrace. There was more that needed to be said between the two of them. It would take effort and patience and understanding to get their relationship back on track. But for now, it was enough to know they loved each other.

# EPILOGUE

### December

"Merry Christmas, Mr. Bedford!" Lyssa Sampson called on her way out of the classroom.

"Merry Christmas, Lyssa. Enjoy the holidays."

"I will." The door swung closed behind her.

Ah, the sudden and very welcome silence.

Al made a quick sweep of the classroom, looking for anything that shouldn't be left behind until school resumed after the new year. Finding nothing out of place, he returned to the front of the classroom. As he bent to retrieve his briefcase, his gaze alighted on the new photograph sitting on his desktop. There they were, the happy Bedford family—Al, Patti, Weston, and Sunni—all of them wearing red and white sweaters. Looking at the photograph made him grin every time.

"Knock, knock."

He turned. "Hey, beautiful."

Patti held the door open wide. "Are you ready to go?"

"I'm ready." He picked up his briefcase.

Twice a month, on the advice of their counselor, Al and Patti left the twins for a few hours with his parents or Miss Hart and Amy Livingston, and they did something fun, just the two of them. Dinner out, a movie, a walk in the park—it didn't matter what they did as long as both considered it fun and they did it together.

This afternoon they were decorating their new home for Christmas. The fifty-year-old house was surrounded by tall trees and mature shrubs, perfect for trimming with strings of lights. There were many couples he knew who wouldn't think hanging Christmas lights a fun activity, but he and Patti were both so glad to be moved into their new home before Christmas, they'd thought it a great idea.

Betty Frazier, their Realtor, said that closing on the sale of their old house and closing on the purchase of their new one so quickly was nothing short of a miracle. Al agreed, especially since they were now debt free, except for their quite reasonable mortgage.

Arriving at the door, he set his briefcase on the floor so he could wrap his wife in his embrace and kiss her soundly. When their lips parted, he said, "I love you."

Three simple words, but they spoke of trust and healing, determination and forgiveness, hopes and dreams. Thanks to wise counsel and a shared faith, they'd weathered the storm that had battered their marriage earlier in the year and come out stronger on the other side. Now he knew that when more trials came, as they did in every life, they would face them together.

With an arm still around Patti's shoulders, Al picked up his briefcase a second time and said, "Honey, let's go home."

# ACKNOWLEDGMENTS

A special thanks to Kris and Susan Livingston, high bidders for the "featured character" prize in the February 2006 "Under Construction" fundraiser on behalf of Cole Valley Christian Schools, Meridian, Idaho. The Livingstons chose to have a *Sweet Dreams Drive* character named for their daughter, Amy.

A student at Cole Valley Christian School, Amy is a good big sister to Beth and enjoys figure skating, dancing, fishing, reading, and singing. She is very creative and one day may write a novel of her own.

Amy, I loved meeting you and your parents. I hope you enjoy seeing your name in print.

Dear Readers:

With *Sweet Dreams Drive*, I bid farewell to my friends in Hart's Crossing. I hope you've enjoyed reading the series and have become as fond of the town's residents as I am. Although Hart's Crossing is fictional, I have known small towns much like it. Places where neighbors care for neighbors and clerks in the grocery store know customers by their first names.

I look forward to writing my next full-length novels. I hope you'll be watching for them. Please visit my website (www.robinleehatcher.com) for the latest information available.

In the grip of his grace,
Robin Lee Hatcher

*From her heart . . . to yours!*

**Robin Lee Hatcher** discovered her vocation as a novelist after many years of reading everything she could put her hands on, including the backs of cereal boxes and ketchup bottles. However, she's certain there are better plots and fewer calories in her books than in puffed rice and hamburgers.

The winner of the Christy Award for Excellence in Christian Fiction, two RITA Awards for Best Inspirational Romance, and the RWA Lifetime Achievement Award, Robin is the author of over fifty books, including *Catching Katie*, named one of the Best Books of 2004 by *Library Journal*.

Robin enjoys being with her family, playing with Poppet (her high maintenance Papillon), spending time in the beautiful Idaho outdoors, reading books that make her cry, and watching romantic movies. She is passionate about the theater, and several nights every summer, she can be found at the outdoor amphitheater of the Idaho Shakespeare Festival, enjoying Shakespeare under the stars. She makes her home in Boise.

Look for these other great stories from

# Hart's Crossing

the small town with a big heart

Legacy Lane

Veterans Way

Sweet Dreams Drive

# Duty brought her home.
## Can love make her stay?

Angie Hunter left Hart's Crossing for college and never looked back. So when her widowed mother needs care following surgery, Angie is more than ready to hire a nurse rather than return to her antiquated hometown. But when she is passed over for a promotion at work, an angry Angie quits and heads home anyway.

Francine Hunter is both excited and nervous about having her daughter home for the next two months. She sees this as her chance to make a new connection with her estranged daughter. Will she be able to nudge Angie toward faith without overdoing it? Or will Angie pick up and leave for a new job as soon as Francine has recovered?

ℜ Revell  |  www.revellbooks.com  |  Available at bookstores everywhere

HART'S CROSSING

ROBIN LEE
HATCHER

*Duty brought her home.*
*Can love make her stay?*

Legacy Lane

Don't miss book 1 in the Hart's Crossing series

# Is it too late for a
## second chance at romance?

Jimmy Scott just moved back to his hometown of Hart's Crossing. And it's just
as he remembered. Then he bumps into an
old friend—Stephanie Watson, a childhood
sweetheart he had once planned on marrying.
As forgotten memories flood back, James
wonders what might have happened if he
hadn't left for the war in Korea. Is it possible
he could still have feelings for this woman?

Stephanie Watson loves this sleepy little
town on the plains of southern Idaho. Between
the Thimbleberry Quilting Club, trips to the
hair parlor, and her grandchildren, she's kept
pretty busy. While surprised by Jimmy's return, she enjoys reminiscing about the good
times they had. But could this friendship be
turning into something more? And could
Stephanie possibly be so lucky as to fall in
love with the same man twice?

HART'S CROSSING

# ROBIN LEE
# HATCHER

*Is it too late for a*
*second chance at romance?*

OVER THE RAINBOW DINER

# Veterans Way

# Could a little innocent scheming bring two hearts together?

Nobody loves baseball more than ten-year-old Lyssa Sampson. Nobody. For as long as she can remember, she's had only one dream: to be a pitcher at the Little League World Series. But Coach Mel Jenkins has other plans, and Lyssa sets her mind to a little innocent scheming to make her dream come true.

When Coach Jenkins appears to be interested in Lyssa's single mother, Terri, Lyssa sees an opportunity for a little matchmaking. Maybe her efforts will help her mother find happiness again—and give Lyssa a chance at her dream at the same time. But will Terri and Mel hit it off? Or will misunderstandings spoil Lyssa's plan?

HART'S CROSSING

# ROBIN LEE HATCHER

*Could a little innocent scheming
bring two hearts together?*

# Diamond Place